Braveheart

Pearson Education Limited
Edinburgh Gate, Harlow,
Essex CM20 2JE, England
and Associated Companies throughout the world.

ISBN 0 582 41680 9

First published in Great Britain by Signet 1995
This adaptation first published by Penguin Books 1996
Published by Addison Wesley Longman Limited and Penguin Books Ltd. 1998
New edition first published 1999

5 7 9 10 8 6 4

Text copyright © Jane Rollason 1996
Illustrations copyright © Icon Productions/Twentieth Century Fox 1996
All rights reserved

The moral right of the adapter has been asserted

Typeset by RefineCatch Limited, Bungay, Suffolk
Set in 11/14pt Monotype Bembo
Printed in Spain by Mateu Cromo, S.A. Pinto (Madrid)

Published by Pearson Education Limited in association with
Penguin Books Ltd., both companies being subsidiaries of Pearson Plc

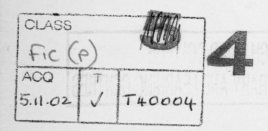

For a complete list of the titles available in the Penguin Readers series please write to your local
Pearson Education office or to: Marketing Department, Penguin Longman Publishing,
80 Strand, London, WC2R 0RL

Introduction

*'Sons of Scotland,' he shouted, 'You have come here to fight as free men.
Yes – if you fight, perhaps you'll die. If you run, you may live for a time.
But at what cost? They'll kill us, but I say we'll always be free!' The
army of Scotsmen answered with one voice. A great shout went up, 'We
will be free!'*

Braveheart is the true story of William Wallace – a young boy
who sees terrible things and grows into a fighter. His story is one
of love for a beautiful and strong Scottish girl and hope for
himself and his country; of rebel attacks and terrible battles; of an
English king who wanted to win Scotland; of the secret meetings
and plans of the nobles of Scotland; and of a beautiful French
princess.

There is a film of *Braveheart* with Mel Gibson as William
Wallace and Sophie Marceau as Princess Isabella. When Mel
Gibson was making the film in Scotland and Ireland, he said,
'This story could happen anywhere.' The film was one of the
most popular films of 1995.

The American writer Randall Wallace first heard about William
Wallace when he visited Edinburgh Castle in Scotland. The
more he knew about William, the more he wanted to tell his
story.

Randall Wallace's family went to America from Ireland and
Scotland many years ago. They were farmers, like the family of
William Wallace, and bought farms in Tennessee in the Ameri-
can South. Randall was born there, but he now lives in southern
California with his wife and two sons.

Braveheart is his fifth novel. He also wrote the words for the
film of *Braveheart*.

v

England and Scotland at the time of William Wallace.

Chapter 1   The Boy

The year was 1276. In a quiet, sunny Scottish valley, a group of
Scottish nobles rode towards a farm. The nobles rode handsome
horses and wore rich clothes. Each noble had a boy with him.
But they carried no weapons because this was a meeting of
truce.

Scotland had no king. The old king died without a son or
daughter. The English king, Edward I, wanted to choose a new
king for Scotland. The Scottish nobles wanted to choose their
ruler. So there was war. The fighting went on and things were
difficult – there was no food because the farmers were fighting
for the nobles. Edward I – 'Longshanks' they called him
because he had long legs – called a truce. The bravest nobles
came, leaving their weapons behind. They came to the meeting place – a large farm building that belonged to a farmer
called MacAndrews. They tied their horses outside and went
in.

One of the neighbouring farmers was a man called Malcolm
Wallace. He was a strong, brave man who wanted Scots to rule
Scotland. He had two sons, John, who was eighteen, and William,
then only seven. William had his father's blue eyes. Malcolm's
wife died when William was born.

Later that same day, Malcolm and John rode off to the
MacAndrews' farm, carrying farm tools with them as weapons.
William watched them. He loved his father and wanted to be like
him. He ran to his horse and rode after them.

They stopped on the hill above the farm.

'Stay here,' Malcolm said to William.

When Malcolm and John arrived at the farm building everything was quiet. No people, no horses. They held their weapons

ready and pushed open the door. They looked up and their hearts stopped. Thirty nobles and thirty boys. And one farmer. All dead. Tied by the neck. They heard a sound behind them and quickly turned. William stood there, looking up at the bodies.

'William! Get out of here!' shouted John.

At first William did not think the bodies were real. Then he touched one and realized. He shut his eyes to the terrible picture and ran this way and that, knocking into bodies. Malcolm caught William and held him.

'English murderers!' he said.

◆

That night a group of local men met at the Wallace farm. William listened from the door.

'The nobles who wanted to fight are dead,' said Malcolm. 'So *we* have to show the English that we won't lie down and serve them. We're not dogs but men!'

They rode off the next day to attack the English. William stayed at home and fought the English in a game with his friend, Hamish. Night came. William watched through a window. His father and brother did not return. But they returned the next morning – Old Campbell, Hamish's father, brought their bodies.

'William . . . Come here, my boy,' said Old Campbell kindly. William looked away and shut his eyes. He looked back, but the bodies of his father and brother were still there.

◆

William stood at the graves and the neighbours looked at the boy. What would happen to him now? A little girl of five with long red hair came towards him. She handed William a flower – the purple flower of Scotland. Their eyes met and then the girl walked back to her mother.

A tall, dark man rode towards the crowd who stood near the graves. William looked at him.

'Uncle Argyle?' William said.

That night the boy and his uncle sat together at the table. Argyle had no wife or children but he would take the boy home with him. Malcolm's sword lay on the table. William tried to lift it.

'First learn to use this,' Argyle said, pointing to William's head, 'and then I will teach you to use that.'

William did not take much with him to Argyle's house – only his mother's wedding dress and his father's sword. When they left the empty farm, he looked back only once.

Chapter 2   The Rebel

Years later, a beautiful young French princess walked through the great rooms of a London castle. She came into a large room. Longshanks, tall and handsome, stood in front of his nobles. He saw Isabella.

'Where is my son?' he shouted. 'I send for him – and he sends you, his new wife! How can the son of the King of England be so weak!' His eyes shone angrily.

He turned back to his nobles. 'I want to rule France. But first I must rule Scotland. Nobles are the key to the Scottish door. We must give land here in England to Scottish nobles. We must give land in the Highlands and Lowlands of Scotland to our own nobles.'

'But our people do not want to live among the Scottish rebels,' said one old noble.

'Then we shall make a better offer. We shall bring back the old rule of "first night" – a girl who lives on a noble's land must spend her wedding night with the noble of the land, not with her husband.'

Longshanks stood in front of his nobles. He saw Isabella. 'Where is my son?' he shouted. 'I send for him — and he sends you, his new wife! How can the son of the King of England be so weak!'

Isabella's blood went cold. She thought of her own wedding night just past. Her new husband did not come to her bedroom — he preferred to be with his friend, Peter. Longshanks looked at her, smiling.

♦

Soon after, many miles north of London, a group of horsemen rode up the hill to Edinburgh Castle. In the centre of the group was a handsome young man on a fine horse. His shoulders were strong and he carried a heavy sword at his side. Robert, 17th Earl of Bruce, was a fighting man.

Twenty-four Scottish nobles, all friends of Robert 'the Bruce', sat round a large table in the central room of the castle. When

Robert came in they were silent. Robert the Bruce wanted to be King of Scotland and these men were on his side. Another Scottish family, the Balliols, also wanted to rule. They had many friends too and there was war between the two families. The Balliols and the Bruces were all brave men but people could not trust them. They looked after themselves first and Scotland second. Sometimes they fought with the English and sometimes against them.

Lord Mornay, a young noble and friend of Robert, spoke. 'The people want us to fight now. They are very angry about this new English rule of "first night".'

'We must wait,' said Robert, 'until we are ready.'

♦

A day's journey from Edinburgh there was a different world. Lanark was a village of rough streets and stone houses, a market for local farmers, a place for people to meet. Today was market day. There was music and dancing. There was good food to eat and beer to drink. English soldiers watched. Market days were good for the English rulers. When the people were enjoying themselves, they were not fighting.

They watched a young man ride into the village. His eyes were blue and his hair was light brown, shining yellow in the sun. He wore a farmer's clothes but he did not look like a farmer. With his straight back, strong body and intelligent face, he looked dangerous. Everyone noticed the new arrival. Old Campbell, his bright red hair now going grey, watched with his old rebel friend, MacClannough. The young man got off his horse and walked through the crowd.

'MacClannough . . .,' Old Campbell said quietly, 'could that be . . . William Wallace?'

Murron MacClannough was also watching. She was now the most beautiful girl in the village, maybe in all of Scotland, with

They watched a young man ride into the village. He wore a farmer's clothes but he did not look like a farmer. He looked dangerous.

her long red hair. She was standing in a group of girls. William saw her. Did he remember her? William started to speak to Murron but just then his old friend Hamish walked up to him. The two men smiled.

'Have you come back to your father's farm?' Hamish asked.

'Yes. Good to see you again,' William said. He shook hands with his father's old friends. It began to rain. Everyone ran inside, but not William. He stood and watched the rain.

That night William stood at the door of the farmhouse and remembered his years there with his father and brother. He looked across the valley at the MacClannough house, friendly through the storm, smoke from the kitchen fire climbing into the sky.

The MacClannoughs were surprised to hear a knock at the door so late. When MacClannough opened the door, there outside in the rain, was William Wallace on his horse.

'Good evening. Can I speak with your daughter?' he asked. 'Murron, would you like to go for a ride on this fine evening?'

Before her parents could say no, Murron jumped up behind William and they disappeared through the trees. They rode up high into the hills. They came to a group of trees. On the other side of the trees the ground fell away below them. They were looking down on a beautiful lake. They stood together and said nothing. William took Murron home. Before he went, he put something in her hand. Then he jumped on his horse and rode away. Murron and her mother looked at the present: a dried flower – the same flower that five-year-old Murron gave to William at his father's grave.

♦

The next day William started work on the farmhouse. He climbed up on the roof to mend some holes where the rain came

Murron jumped up behind William and they rode up high into the hills.

in. MacClannough rode up and asked William to come to a meeting – a secret meeting. They rode together deep into the hills. There they met with twenty men, all farmers.

'We put ourselves in danger to bring you here, because you are the son of Malcolm Wallace. Do you understand?'

'I do,' William answered. He knew rebels when he saw them.

'Every day the English send in more soldiers. When Malcolm Wallace was alive, we met here for every attack,' Old Campbell explained. 'You have come back and we ask ourselves, "Are we still men?" Will you be one of us?'

'I came home to be a farmer and to have a family,' said William. He looked at Old Campbell and Hamish and walked away to the horses. On the way home, he stopped and looked at the graves of his father and brother for a long time.

♦

William did not see Murron for two weeks. Then there was a wedding in the village. Helen MacClannough, a cousin of Murron, was marrying a local boy, Robbie. Everyone came. There was plenty of food, beautiful wild flowers and happy music.

The new husband and wife and their families and friends came out of the church. The wedding party began. Suddenly there was the noise of horses. An English noble rode towards them at the head of a group of English soldiers. The villagers went quiet. The nobleman, Lord Bottoms, was about fifty, grey-haired and fat, with a red face.

'These lands belong to me,' he said. 'And by the rule of "first night", I am here to take this young woman to my bed on the night of her wedding.' No one moved.

'No, by God!' shouted Helen's father.

The soldiers were ready for this. In a second their swords were pointing down at Helen's father and Robbie. The men wanted to fight, but Helen held onto them tightly.

'I prefer to spend one night with this man than lose both of you for ever,' she said. Then one of the soldiers pulled her up onto his horse behind him and the group rode away.

◆

William and Murron went again to the group of trees in the hills that night. They sat together above the lake and thought of Helen on her wedding night. They talked about their love and their hopes. They kissed long and hard.

'I want to marry you,' said William. 'But no Englishman will take you on our wedding night.'

◆

They married secretly in an old, empty church. Murron gave William a white handkerchief with the flower of Scotland on it. They spent their wedding night under the stars. For the next six weeks they met when they could at night and sometimes in the day. But they did not show that they were husband and wife. When Murron was having a baby they would be safe from Lord Bottoms. Then they would explain to their friends about the secret wedding.

◆

They were both in Lanark one market day. Their eyes met but they did not speak. William walked on. Some English soldiers were sitting at a table and drinking quite near. They watched Murron, who was now more beautiful than ever, buying some bread. She was walking past when one of them suddenly caught her wrist and threw her to the ground. 'Where are you going, my lovely?' he asked.

The other soldiers laughed. He fell on top of her and pulled at her clothes. Murron bit him hard and tried to get away. Suddenly William was there and he caught the soldier's arm from behind.

He threw him into his friends and turned the table over on top of them. One of the soldiers began to shout, 'Rebels! Rebels!' Other soldiers came running. The villagers tried to stop them.

'Run, William, run!' they shouted.

'Are you all right, Murron?' William asked. 'Take the horse and go. I'll meet you at our group of trees.'

William fought off two more soldiers. He watched Murron escape. Then he ran off through the crowd, in and out of the narrow streets. Soldiers were everywhere. Hesselrig, head of the English soldiers, arrived, too late. William escaped into the trees and disappeared. He thought Murron was free. But Murron did not escape . . . She fell from her horse and the soldiers caught her.

William arrived at the group of trees in the hills. 'Murron!' he called softly. And then again more loudly. 'Murron!' he shouted. But there was no answer.

Murron was in prison. Hesselrig looked at her proud eyes. 'Why isn't she afraid of me? She's just a girl,' he thought to himself. 'And who is this man who can fight six of my soldiers at the same time and beat them?' he asked.

'His name is William Wallace,' one of the soldiers answered. 'He has a farm along the valley. Let's burn it.'

'I want *him*, not his farm. And he wants *you*, my beautiful girl. And you will bring him to *us*!'

Hesselrig took Murron into the village square and tied her to a tree. The villagers came to watch.

'An attack on the king's soldiers is an attack on the king . . . and this is what happens,' he shouted. He calmly walked up to Murron, took out his knife and cut her throat. Blood ran from the cut and she was dead.

◆

William found his friends at Old Campbell's farm.

'Have you seen Murron?' he asked them. 'She got away. I saw

11

Murron did not escape . . . She fell from her horse and the soldiers caught her.

her! I saw her!' William searched their faces. Old Campbell told William that Murron was dead. William could see that he was not lying. He went outside. The moon shone on the purple flowers among the grass. William's wild screams, angry and sad, cut through the black night.

William Wallace jumped on the nearest horse and rode to his farm. He took his father's great sword from its hiding place. The rebels followed. All through the valley people took up their weapons and ran behind him towards Lanark, where Hesselrig and his men were waiting. Wallace rode on. He stopped in front of the line of soldiers just outside the village. He was not afraid. He was ready to kill.

The battle was short. No one could stop Wallace and his angry followers. English soldiers lay dead everywhere. Wallace found Hesselrig and pulled him out by his hair to the square. His wild eyes looked at the face of Murron's murderer. He took his sword and cut Hesselrig's throat in one movement. The people were shouting, 'Wal-lace! Wal-lace!' But he did not hear them. He looked at Murron's blood on the ground, he looked at the blood of the Englishman on his sword. He knew he would fight as a rebel from this day until he died.

◆

Lord Bottoms sat on his horse outside his castle. He was getting his men ready to find the rebels and to kill William Wallace as an example to the people of Scotland. He gave a soldier a letter to take to the Lord Governor at Stirling Castle. But the soldier did not get past the castle walls. Wallace and his men were waiting outside. Suddenly there were Scots everywhere. Bottoms tried to shout orders. The rebels pulled him from his fine horse. Wallace tied his hands and threw him onto an old and tired horse.

'Go back to England. Tell them that Wallace is a free man of

Scotland. Our sons and daughters belong to us, not to the king of England. Tell them . . . Scotland is free!'

♦

They put Murron in the ground the next day. They cut a flower of Scotland into the stone by her grave. William put the white handkerchief next to his broken heart.

♦

Far off in London, Princess Isabella sat in the castle with her friend, Nicolette. She watched Prince Edward playing ball games with his friends in the garden. Nicolette told her news of Scotland and the story of William and Murron. This was the kind of man Isabella would like for a husband.

At that moment Longshanks arrived. 'You play games here, boy?' he shouted at his son. 'The rebels are attacking our soldiers in Scotland! They have sent Lord Bottoms back to England!' He knocked Edward to the ground. 'I'm going to France now. I'm leaving Scotland to you. Do you understand?' He pulled Edward up by the throat. 'And turn yourself into a man.' The king left.

♦

Back in Scotland, Robert the Bruce sat with his father. 'It's time to fight like William Wallace. All Scotland is with him. This is no time to talk with the English,' said the young Robert.

'Fighting is not enough. Yes, Wallace is brave. But a dog is brave. You're noble. You are clever and brave. We'll go with these rebels on our lands in Scotland. But we'll stand against them on our lands in the south. Longshanks will do anything to rule Scotland. We will, too.'

♦

Nicolette told Isabella news of Scotland and the story of William and Murron. This was the kind of man Isabella would like for a husband.

William sat near a small fire, thinking. The ground was wet from days of rain but with the trees above their heads, they were dry enough. Hamish looked into the dark forest round them, his eyes searching for movement. Old Campbell was mending weapons. Guards were standing further away.

'What do we do when Longshanks sends all of his northern army against us?' William asked.

'That's a good question,' answered Old Campbell. 'They have many horses and new weapons. We have only swords and weapons that we make on our farms.'

'They'll ride right over us,' said Hamish.

'So we fight the Highland way,' said Old Campbell. 'Attack and run into the hills. Burn everything on the way.'

'Then it is our own land and villages that we burn. But could we beat Longshanks's army?' William looked up at the trees and

William looked up at the trees and thought. 'I want the men to make a hundred spears. Each spear will be twice as tall as a man.'

thought. 'I want the men to make a hundred spears. Each spear will be twice as tall as a man.'

Before Hamish could ask William any more questions, the guards brought in some new rebels. Men came from all over Scotland every day to fight with William Wallace. But any one of them could be a spy for Longshanks.

The new men looked at William Wallace and their faces shone. William was dirty like the others, and his hair was wet and full of leaves, but they saw the fire inside him. It was that fire that they wanted to follow. Among the new rebels was a handsome young man from Ireland called Stephen. William spoke to them all.

'Show us that you can live without food and sleep and then you can fight for us.'

◆

A hundred English horsemen rode in straight lines across open country. Lord Dolecroft rode in front. They were looking for William Wallace and his rebels. Sometimes they came very close. They found fires still smoking. But they never saw them, until one day when they saw Hamish and a group of rebels near some trees. The Scots saw the horsemen and ran like frightened animals.

'After them!' Dolecroft shouted and kicked his horse. They followed Hamish and his hungry and tired men across an open field with low hills all round.

'Now we have them,' shouted Dolecroft. He rode into the field but the ground was very wet and the horses' legs disappeared up to their knees. Suddenly there were Scots everywhere, waving swords above their heads. William Wallace gave the order to attack. Every Englishman died.

◆

The news of Wallace's win over the English travelled quickly. The rebels hid in an empty farm building. The farmer was friendly and gave them food and clothes.

William slept while Old Campbell and Stephen talked about battles and how to win them. Hamish came in.

'News has arrived,' he called softly. William woke up. 'The English are sending a great army to Stirling Castle. Some say there are ten thousand, some say twenty! And the Scots are coming down from the Highlands. Hundreds of them!'

◆

Stirling Castle stood high on a hill above open country. A river cut through the field in front of it. A wooden bridge crossed the river in front of the castle.

On 17 June, 1297, a group of Scottish nobles stood on a smaller hill looking down on to the field, ready for battle. Robert the Bruce was in prison so Lord Mornay took his place at the head of the Scottish army. From the other side of the bridge they watched the great English army moving.

'It looks like twenty thousand!' shouted Lochlan, another noble. 'But our spies say it is ten thousand.'

'And we have only two thousand!' said Mornay. The nobles did not think there would be a battle. They were ready to make a truce with the English. The English army stood in front of the castle walls and along the river. They were in straight lines – foot soldiers with swords at the front, horsemen with spears at the back. Their weapons were new and shining. The Scots had leather shirts and farm tools.

'So many!' said one young soldier, looking over the river.

'If the nobles make a truce, they'll send us home,' replied an old soldier standing next to him. 'If not, we'll attack. They'll stay on their hill and we'll die. They'll ride home and call themselves brave.'

'I don't want to fight so that they can have more land!'

'Neither do I,' said the old one, and he turned and walked away from the battle towards home. Others followed, first one by one and then in groups. Lochlan shouted at them to stop but they did not listen.

'Why do they have to die for us?' said Mornay.

But suddenly they did stop. William Wallace rode into the middle of the Scots army with his rebels, his fair hair flying in the wind, his strong arms showing under his ordinary leather shirt. He rode up to the nobles.

'This is our army,' said Lochlan. 'Do you want to serve?'

'If this is your army, why are the men leaving? I serve Scotland, not you.' He turned his horse to look at the men.

'We didn't come to fight for them!' shouted the old soldier. And another man called, 'Home! The English are too many! We'll all die.'

Wallace held up his hand to speak and the army was silent. 'Sons of Scotland!' he shouted. 'I am William Wallace. You have come here to fight as free men. Yes – if you fight, perhaps you'll die. If you run, you may live for a time. But at what cost? Perhaps they'll kill us, but I say we'll always be free!' The army of Scotsmen answered with one voice. A great shout went up, 'We will be free!'

'Fine words,' said Stephen, coming up behind Wallace. 'Now what do we do?'

'Follow our plan. Bring out the spears. Put them in the front line,' ordered Wallace. Then he rode with Lochlan and Mornay to talk to the English. They met on the bridge. Lord Talmadge, head of the English army, made an offer. 'The king will give you lands in York –' he began. Wallace stopped him.

'I have an offer for *you*,' he said. 'Take your army straight back to England. Ask every Scots man, woman and child on the way to forgive you for one hundred years of murder and stealing.

*The army of Scotsmen answered with one voice. A great shout went up,
'We will be free!'*

Then perhaps you and your men will live. If not, every one of you will die today!'

Wallace turned to Lochlan and Mornay. 'Be ready. Follow my orders,' he told them. He rode back to the army and they followed.

The English quickly moved their horses across the bridge. They lined up opposite the Scots. Then the English foot soldiers began to cross behind them.

The English horsemen stood tall and proud; their horses were in purple and red. No one could beat them. Talmadge ordered them to attack. The Scots stood and waited. The English horses came at them, nearer and nearer.

'Wait . . .,' shouted Wallace. 'Wait . . . NOW!'

Wallace's men brought out their secret weapons – long spears, each one twice as tall as a man. They pointed them at the horses. The English could not stop their horses and their swords were too short. The long spears cut the men and horses to pieces. Everyone on the battlefield listened to the screams of the dying English.

The English pushed their foot soldiers across the bridge. Following Wallace's orders, Lord Mornay rode with his horsemen away from the battle. The English saw Mornay leave and thought now they would win.

Wallace lifted his sword. 'For Scotland!' he screamed. He ran towards the English, his brave rebels behind him. They attacked and killed all the soldiers in the field and then pushed onto the bridge. More English soldiers were still trying to get onto the bridge from the other side. The Scots caught the men in the middle and cut them down. The water below the bridge was red with blood. The English began to realize that they could not win. Some stayed and fought bravely but others turned and ran, among them Lord Talmadge. Just at that moment, Mornay and his men attacked the English from the side. The river was easy to

Wallace's men brought out their secret weapons — long spears,
each one twice as tall as a man. They pointed them at the horses.

cross on horseback behind the trees to the east. The English
ran, trying to escape the Scottish swords. The terrible Battle of
Stirling was finished. The Scots lifted Wallace up onto their
shoulders. The nobles and ordinary Scotsmen shouted with one
voice, 'Wal-lace! Wal-lace! WAL-LACE!'

◆

On a field in northern France, the English king was angry. His
army was fighting a long, slow war against the French. 'Why
aren't we already in Paris? We'll have to spend the winter here
now.'

'We cannot,' answered General Peters bravely. 'Half the men
will die of cold and hunger.'

'We'll bring our army from Scotland here in the spring,' said
Longshanks, but just then a rider arrived. He was tired and dirty.

He handed the king a letter. Longshanks read the letter. Suddenly, his face looked old and grey. 'We have no army in Scotland,' he said quietly.

Chapter 3   First Lord of Scotland

After the Battle of Stirling, William Wallace was famous all over Scotland. He rode into Edinburgh and up to the castle, his friends at his side. The people looked at him with wide eyes like children. The nobles in their fine clothes did not understand how an ordinary man could win a great battle like that, when the Bruces and Balliols could not. Robert the Bruce was now out of prison and he stood among the other nobles as William walked into the castle. He could see at once that this Wallace would never serve any other man. A man began to read: 'In the name of God, Sir William Wallace, we make you First Lord of Scotland!' They gave him a gold ring of office and the nobles went down on their knees.

Maybe William could be First Lord but he could not be king because he was not a nobleman. William watched as the nobles immediately began to fight among themselves. They wanted to find a king, but still they could not agree. William turned and walked away.

'Sir William!' one noble cried. 'Where are you going?'

He turned back, his eyes burning with anger. 'We have beaten the English! But they'll come back, because *you* won't stand together.' William looked at Robert the Bruce as he spoke. 'There's only one side to be on – not the Bruces, not the Balliols, but the side of the Scottish people. We must fight so that the people can be free.'

'What will you do?' another noble asked.

'I'll take the fighting into England and beat the English on

'In the name of God, Sir William Wallace, we make you First Lord
of Scotland!'

their own land!' said William. He looked round at the open mouths of the nobles and left the castle.

◆

A few weeks later, far away in London, Prince Edward and his friend Peter, listened, afraid. Doors crashed open and walls shook. Longshanks was back from France. He arrived in Edward's rooms, high up in the castle, and looked at the two young men with cold, black eyes.

'What is the news from the north?' he asked angrily.

'Nothing to report, Father,' said Edward.

'What? A bunch of rebels beats our army at Stirling and you say "nothing to report"!' The king's face burned angrily.

'I have ordered more men to serve as soldiers,' said Edward. 'We'll have a large army by the spring. We know from my cousin, the Governor of York, that Wallace is near York now. But the winter is coming. The Scots will have empty stomachs and they'll be weak. We'll catch this Wallace and tie him up by his neck in front of his rebels!'

A man came in with a letter.

'Give it to me!' the prince ordered proudly. He was beginning to feel strong. The feeling did not last. He read the letter and his face went white.

'Wallace has taken York,' he said slowly.

'Impossible!' shouted Longshanks. The man also carried a bag which he placed on a table. Edward looked in it and jumped back, shaking. Longshanks opened the bag and took out the bloody head of the Governor of York, his own brother's son. He dropped the head back into the bag.

'What animal would do this?' said Peter quickly. 'We shall stop him if he comes south of York!'

Longshanks did not answer. He looked at Edward. 'Who is this who speaks before I ask him to?' Before Edward could answer, Longshanks took Peter by the throat and threw him out of the window. Peter screamed just before he hit the ground. Edward ran to the window and looked down at Peter's body. Peter was the only person that he loved and trusted and now his body was broken and bloody on the stones far below. He took a knife from his jacket and ran at his father. Longshanks smiled. At last his son was fighting for himself. His smile disappeared, and he took hold of his son and kicked him until he was almost dead.

'We must make a truce with the Scots,' said Longshanks, feeling nothing for his son lying on the ground. 'But who should go? Not this weak son of mine. Not me. I do not want my head brought to London in a bag. Who can I send?'

◆

The Scots army were resting outside York. They mended their clothes and weapons. William, Hamish and Stephen were in the Governor's rooms in the city, studying his papers. Old Campbell hurried in, almost too excited to speak. 'A group of Longshanks's men are here. They want to make a truce. Be careful, William, perhaps they want to kill you.'

'I hope they do,' said Stephen, putting on his leather jacket. 'I haven't killed an Englishman for five days.'

When William and his six riders arrived at the meeting place, they found French guards outside the English tent.

'Longshanks! I have come!' William shouted at the entrance.

The guards pulled back the sides of the tent door and there in the shadows stood a tall woman in fine clothes. William began to shake. Hamish looked at Old Campbell. She was just like Murron! And when she moved towards them and into the light, she was more like her.

'I am the Princess of Wales,' she said. 'Wife of the king's son. I come from the king and I speak for him.'

'I am the Princess of Wales,' Isabella said. 'Wife of the king's son.
I come from the king and I speak for him.' William looked at her
and thought of his lost love.

William looked at her and thought of his lost love.

Isabella saw in him everything she wanted in a man. He was tall and strong, his hair was wild and his eyes were soft. Here was a man who could win battles, a man that armies would follow. And yet he could ride away from it all and it would not matter to him. William got off his horse. In his eyes Isabella saw something new in the face of a man — a deep sadness. And she knew that it was for Murron.

'It's battle that I want, not talk,' said William.

'But now that I am here, will you speak with a woman?' She went into the tent and he followed her. Inside were Nicolette and Lord Hamilton, one of Longshanks's men.

'I understand that you are now First Lord of Scotland,' the princess began. 'Did God tell you to kill the good people of York?'

'We attacked York because every English attack on Scotland starts from there!' said William.

'. . . And to cut off the head of my husband's cousin?'

'Your husband's cousin found and murdered all the Scottish women and children in York before we attacked. They threw more than one hundred dead people over the city walls!'

'That is not possible.' Isabella went white and looked at Hamilton. She saw that it was true.

'He's lying,' said Hamilton, speaking to her in Latin.

When William answered them in Latin, they both jumped in surprise. And then he spoke in French. 'Ask your king who is lying.'

The princess asked Nicolette and Hamilton to wait outside. She made the king's offer of land and money. Wallace turned to leave. Isabella spoke quietly so that no one could hear. 'I know your story. I know of Murron.'

'She was my wife,' William said just as softly. Suddenly

he wanted to talk and he told her of Murron, of everything that happened many years before in the MacAndrews' farm building when he and his father found thirty murdered Scottish nobles.

'You are strong inside like Murron. You will be a good queen. Tell your king that he will never rule William Wallace. He will not rule any Scot while I live.'

◆

William walked through the empty streets of York that night. When the sun started to come up, he returned to Hamish and the others. Their fire was still burning.

'Want some food?' Hamish asked.

William shook his head. 'No word from Edinburgh?'

'Yes.' Hamish waited for a few seconds and then went on. 'They're not sending any more men, William.'

'They know about York! And they won't send more soldiers!' William looked at the fire. 'If I take this army to London, half the men will die of illness or hunger on the way. We must go back to Scotland. But we have not finished yet.'

◆

In London Isabella reported on her meeting with Wallace. She listened to the king talking about his plans. Soldiers were already on their way from Wales and France. And with terrible new weapons that could cut through metal like a knife through butter. She realized that the king did not want a truce. Her words to William Wallace were lies. The king used her to win time. And now his soldiers were getting ready to attack the Scots army from the sides and from behind. She returned to her rooms, shaking angrily and thinking of a plan.

'I will send Nicolette to my castle in the north,' she thought.

'On the way, she can find Wallace and his men. She can tell them the king's plans.'

♦

The Battle of Falkirk was more terrible than Stirling. Of all the Scottish nobles, only Mornay was there with a hundred riders. Robert the Bruce did not come.

The famous Scottish spears lined up. The English horses began the attack from the right. The English foot soldiers shot their terrible new weapons at the spearmen from the left. Wallace ordered Mornay to attack the foot soldiers before they could shoot again. Mornay did not attack.

From the English side Longshanks watched Mornay riding away from the battle with his men. The English nobles turned to their king in surprise. Longshanks explained. 'His payment is new land in England and Scotland.'

William felt helpless. With Mornay gone, no one was guarding the spearmen. The English foot soldiers shot again, their terrible weapons cutting the Scottish spearmen to pieces. The rest of the Scottish army did not wait for orders. They ran screaming towards the English. The battle was long and hard. Soldiers on both sides fought bravely. But there were too many English.

Towards the end of the battle the English horsemen attacked again. Wallace saw them coming. He pulled the first rider to the ground. It was Robert the Bruce, fighting for the English! Wallace looked at his face. In that second he realized that there was no hope for Scotland. He felt weak. The Bruce waved his sword at Wallace.

'Fight me! Fight me!' he shouted. But Wallace could not fight now. He took the gold ring of office off his finger and threw it at Robert the Bruce's feet. Stephen rode up quickly. He pulled William up behind him onto his horse and the two rode away from the battle.

*From the English side Longshanks watched Mornay riding away
from the battle with his men. 'His payment is new land in England
and Scotland.'*

The battle was long and hard. Soldiers on both sides fought bravely.
But there were too many English.

Robert the Bruce watched Wallace escape. He looked at the ground and saw the blood of his countrymen. 'I will never fight on the wrong side again,' he said.

◆

A few days later William was at Murron's grave. Rain fell hard on his face. He held in his shaking hand the white handkerchief – something from a better world.

Rain was falling in London too. Longshanks was smiling. 'All the Scottish nobles have agreed to serve me as their king. Now we can send soldiers from Scotland to fight in our armies in France. Well, my flower,' he said, turning to Isabella, 'we have seen the last of your Wallace, I think.' She looked out of the window, her eyes as wet as the rain.

Chapter 4   Brave Heart

William spent some months in France and Italy asking for help for Scotland from the King of France and the Pope. He returned to Scotland with empty hands: they would not help.

◆

Lord Mornay lay in bed looking out from the window of his high room at his rich land. When he slept, his head was full of pictures of William Wallace – running towards him at Falkirk with his sword held high and murder in his eyes.

Suddenly Mornay heard the sound of a horse, not outside the castle but *inside*. Impossible. Surely he was asleep. Then he heard shouts, too, and screams from below. Then silence, and then a sudden great crash. William Wallace rode into his bedroom. Mornay never spoke again. Wallace cut through his neck with one quick movement. The guards at the door stood with their mouths open.

Wallace threw a jacket over his horse's head. He kicked the animal hard. The horse jumped, crashed through the window and horse and rider sailed through the air, down, down, past the castle walls and into the lake below. They swam to land. Wallace got on his horse and rode away. From behind him came the shouts, 'Wal-lace! Wal-lace!'

◆

Isabella found Longshanks and Edward in the castle garden. 'You smile! You have heard the news? The rebels are starting to fight again in Scotland,' said Edward.

'I smile because I have a plan to catch your Wallace.' She spoke to the king. 'Send me to my castle in the north to speak for you. Wallace trusts me. Find thirty of your best killers. I will find a place for a meeting. He will come to the meeting and we will kill him. Easy!'

Longshanks, now old and weak, studied her strong face. 'You see, my stupid son, I have found you a real queen.'

◆

Hamish and Stephen brought William the news. 'Longshanks has sent the princess to make a truce.'

'And where does she want to meet?' asked William.

'It's very strange – in the MacAndrews' farm building!'

William and his friends arrived at the farm building. Wallace handed his sword to Hamish so that everyone in the building could see. The killers waited inside, their knives ready. Wallace came up to the guards outside the door. Suddenly he pushed them inside and shut the doors. Rebels ran out of the woods and put great pieces of wood against the building. Then they burned it to the ground.

Isabella could see the fire from the walls of her castle. A single rider came up to the castle. She sat and waited. After a while, she heard a small noise outside the window. In one quick movement William pulled himself through the narrow window and into the room.

'I understood at once,' he said. 'The MacAndrews' farm. You remembered the story I told you of when I was a boy.'

'I am so pleased to see you,' said Isabella, softly touching his face. 'I know that when you looked at me . . . you saw her.' He turned away.

'You must forgive how I feel,' she said. 'No man has ever looked at me as you do. A queen must love her husband but she must also give him a child. With my husband I cannot do both. Just think,' she went on, 'maybe you'll never be King of Scotland. But perhaps one day your blood will run through the King of England.'

'I cannot love you because of Longshanks,' he said.

'No. But you can love me . . . just because I love you.'

Early the next morning Wallace quietly said goodbye to Isabella.

Early the next morning Wallace quietly said goodbye to Isabella.

He quickly found his rebel friends, Hamish and Stephen. They saw he was full of fire again. The three of them began attacking English soldiers where they could find them. For two days they did not rest.

◆

The Scottish nobles now wanted a meeting with Wallace. They said that they wanted to serve him and not Longshanks.

'Why do you trust them?' asked Hamish, shaking his head. 'You know they will give you to Longshanks.'

'You are probably right. But we can't win without them, Hamish. Standing together is the only hope for our people.'

'I don't want to die. I want to live!' shouted Hamish.

'So do I. I want a home and children. I've asked God for these things. But He has brought me this sword. And if He wants me to die for my country, then I will.'

The three rode to the meeting place. On the way William gave his knife to Stephen and his sword to Hamish. He felt that he was seeing them for the last time.

'Here he is,' said Robert the Bruce, looking through a window. 'And he has no sword. My God, he has a brave heart.'

William came into the house. He looked into the eyes of Robert the Bruce. The two men now saw the same picture – a free Scotland. William held out his hand towards Robert the Bruce.

In seconds there were English soldiers everywhere. 'Noooo!!' screamed Robert the Bruce, who knew nothing of this plan. They tied William up like an animal, took him to London over the back of a horse and threw him in prison.

◆

Longshanks was very ill – he was dying. He could not speak with his voice, only with his eyes. Isabella went to see him. She pulled

'Before you die, listen to this — your blood dies with you. A child who has the blood of William Wallace is growing inside me!'

him close to her by his hair and spoke so softly in his ear that Edward could not hear.

'You see? We all die. Wallace will die tomorrow. But before *you* die, listen to this – your blood dies with you. A child who has the blood of William Wallace is growing inside me!'

◆

William Wallace died slowly in front of a great crowd on 23 August, 1305. They did terrible things to his body so that he would ask for forgiveness, but he would not. In the last seconds of his life he saw Hamish and Stephen in the crowd. And behind them, Murron. For a moment he felt strong. And he cried out, 'WE WILL BE FREE!'

ACTIVITIES

Chapters 1–2

Before you read

1 Look at the map at the beginning of the book. What do you know about Scotland? Have you ever been there? What is the country and the weather like? What do you know about the people and the language? Tell another student.

2 Look at the pictures in the book. What kind of story do you think it is? The most important person in the story is William Wallace. Can you find him in the pictures?

3 Find these words in your dictionary.
   a weapons/battle
   b army/beat
   c spears/sword

   All the words are about fighting. Write three sentences with the words.

4 Find these words in your dictionary.

   castle   grave   noble   rebel   truce   trust

   Now use the words to complete these sentences.
   a When both sides want to stop fighting, they make a . . . . . .
   b A . . . . . is someone who fights against the king or queen.
   c A . . . . . was a very rich man with a lot of land.
   d When someone dies their body is put in a . . . . . .
   e The king and queen sometimes live in a . . . . . near London.
   f It is difficult to . . . . . somebody who lies to you.

After you read

5 Find description on the right for each name on the left.
   a William   A Scottish nobleman
   b Robert the Bruce   William's uncle
   c Isabella   The English king
   d Longshanks   Malcolm's youngest son
   e Murron MacClannough   A French princess
   f Argyle   William's young wife

6 Put these sentences in the right order.

    a William Wallace decides to fight as a rebel.

    b The Scots win the battle at Stirling.

    c Malcolm and John are killed.

    d Murron is murdered by the English soldiers.

    e William Wallace marries Murron.

Chapter 3

Before you read

    7 Look at the picture on page 24. What do you think is going to happen to William Wallace? Do you think the Scots will beat the English again? Why/why not?

After you read

    8 In these pairs of people, what does the first person feel about the second?

        a Longshanks and Prince Edward

        b William Wallace and Princess Isabella

        c Princess Isabella and William Wallace

        d Princess Isabella and Longshanks

        e William Wallace and Robert the Bruce

    9 Work with another student. Have a conversation.

    Student A: You are William Wallace. Tell Student B about your wife, Murron. How did you meet? What happened to her?

    Student B: You are Princess Isabella. Ask Student B questions about Murron.

Chapter 4

Before you read

    10 At the end of Chapter 3, Princess Isabella feels very sad. Look at the picture on page 35. What do you think is going to happen to William Wallace and Isabella? Do you think the story will have a happy ending? Why/why not?

After you read

11 Who says these words? Who to?

    a 'You see, my stupid son, I have found you a real queen.'

    b 'You remembered the story I told you of when I was a boy.'

    c 'But you can love me . . . just because I love you.'

    d 'My God, he has a brave heart.'

    e 'We will be free!'

12 Can you think of a modern country or region which wants to rule itself but does not? What problems do they have?

Writing

13 You live in London in the time of William Wallace. There are no newspapers but you write reports for other people to read. Choose one of the fights or battles in *Braveheart* and write a report about it.

14 It is a year after William Wallace's death. Princess Isabella has had her baby. Write a letter from Isabella to a friend. Tell her about the baby and what your life is like now.

15 Think of a well-known person from your country's past. Find out about him or her. Then write about his/her life.

16 Who did you like most in this story? And who didn't you like? Why?

Answers for the Activities in this book are published in our free resource packs for teachers, the Penguin Readers Factsheets, or available on a separate sheet. Please write to your local Pearson Education office or to: Marketing Department, Penguin Longman Publishing, 80 Strand, London WC2R 0RL